D1590761

The Conjuring

N.K. Aning

Published by N.K. Aning, 2017.

This is a work of fiction. Similarities to real people, places, or events are entirely coincidental.

THE CONJURING

First edition. October 30, 2017.

Copyright © 2017 N.K. Aning.

ISBN: 978-1393252702

Written by N.K. Aning.

Also by N.K. Aning

The Bronze Man's Secret
Damned
Prophecy
The Conjuring
In Her Eyes
The Addiction
The God Dilemma
Jack and God
Jason And The Great Dragon
A Song for Eyram
The Infernal Jury
Pierce and the City of Imaginaterium

Watch for more at https://web.facebook.com/
N-K-Aning-879564645456623/?view_public_for=879564645456623.

To my readers, enjoy the ride while it lasts.

ONE

Lightning streaked across the sky as Milton stood under the canopy gazing over the service that was taking place. His brother, Josh, stood by his side, his body being wracked with silent sobs. Milton's red rimmed eyes were covered by dark glasses. He let his eyes roam over the gathering. His parent's coffin lay in the grave as Father Grant, the parish priest said the last farewells. He had not been listening to the message being preached. *Something about an afterlife*, he thought. Milton spied Carol beside Mark. Despite his grief, his heart skipped a beat when he saw her standing there.

"Dust to dust." The priest enunciated as a slight drizzle began. Milton winced at the pain throbbing in his arm. His hand was in a tourniquet. His other arm was around Josh. He kept whispering to his brother. "It's going to be alright." He didn't believe in the words himself. The crowd broke up at the priest's last words. Milton stood there, waiting to shake hands with the sympathizers. An elderly couple came over and shook his hands. He hardly knew them. He wasn't a regular in church. He spotted Carol making her way towards him. Despite the somber mood he was in, his heart walloped against his chest. Milton chided himself for being excited. Carol's dark dress billowed around her as she stood before him.

"Hey!" Milton said, a wide grin on his face. He immediately wiped it off his face when he saw a neighbor scowling at him. They probably wanted him to play sad all his life.

"Are you going to be ok?" Carol said as she pulled her sash tighter around her shoulder.

"Yeah." Milton said, pulling Josh closer. Carol ruffled Josh's hair. She patted his arm and turned round, heading towards her boyfriend's car. He watched Carol get into Mark's car and drove away. Milton knew he shouldn't feel this way about her, but he couldn't help it. Milton scanned around. The crowd was thinning. Josh sniffed beside him. He hadn't spoken since they started the ceremony.

"We are going to be okay, right?" Josh asked as he stared into his elder brother's eyes. Milton felt a lump in his throat. Those eyes reminded him so much of his dad. He nodded at Josh. Words stuck in his throat. He felt the burden of responsibility on his shoulders all too well. His eyes scanned the grave yard and settled on the newly dug grave pit. The two coffins were lying side by side. It shouldn't have been like this. He wiped a lone tear from his eyes. Someone cleared his throat behind him. Milton glanced back to see Father Grant waiting patiently by his Mustang. The church had borne the expenses for the funeral. For that he was grateful. He waved them over.

"Come on, Josh. Let's go." Milton said as he gently tugged Josh along. They approached the priest who had a solemn look on his face. Overhead, the sun had peeked behind the clouds. The rain had stopped. Father Grant nodded at them and stepped behind the driving wheel. Milton let Josh enter the back seat. He felt a tiny breeze across his face and glanced in the rear view mirror. Beside his parent's pit, he saw the grave workers filling the pit with sand. He entered the car and it drove them off, against the back drop of the heaving and grunting of the graveyard workers. Day one in the life of the orphans had just began. A rueful smile was on his face as he thought of life ahead.

TWO

Milton glanced at the wall clock in his tiny room. It was past his wake up time, but he still lay on his back on his creaking bed. He could hear Josh's snoring on the other bed. Josh had cried himself to sleep the night before. Milton on the other hand had sat in their living room. Reclining on the sofa, reflecting on life ahead. Father Grant had promised the church would assist them. As much as he knew they needed help, he hated handouts. Dad had pummeled that into his skull. Dad, with his litany, "A man must sweat for his keep." As he scrapped his favorite knife over a sharpening stone. Such memories brought tears to his eyes. He debated the merit of staying in bed doing nothing. Finally, common sense overtook tired flesh.

Milton leapt out of his bed and landed on his discarded cloth from last night. He picked them up and threw them onto the equally rumpled bed. House cleaning would come later. The distant relatives had all gone. Now it was up to him and Josh. He stepped out, feet kicking an empty bottle rolling down the grass. He scanned round, taking in the piles of rubbish he was going to clean up. He spied a car revving up. That was certainly their next door neighbor off to work. Milton's contract of employment had expired two weeks earlier. He stepped back into the house. His stomach rumbled as he thought about the prospect of food. Outside, he could hear the blaring of someone's woofer. Time to get some stuff from the garage.

Milton stood in the garage staring at the emptiness of the place. The old tires and skid marks were visible on the floor. Memories flashed by. "Give me the pincers, Milton." His dad would say to him as he peeked under the Toyota's hood. His dad smelling of oil and grease would grin at him. Those were the moments Milton cherished the most. He felt the memories crashing him. Milton gasped for breath as that fateful memory popped up in his mind. The tears came unbidden as he recalled every terrible detail.

THREE

It had been a Saturday. His dad was in the front seat of the Toyota whistling to an oldie from Bob Marley. Mom, was sitting at the front as always, applying makeup. They had just returned from a church programme. Milton had been reluctant to attend the service. His interest in church activities had been waning.

"Milton, you need to take church serious." His dad said as he burped the horn on a taxi in front of them. They had been travelling on the Tema motorway. Cars were speeding past them. Milton rolled his eyes at his dad's comment.

"I don't like going to confession, Mom." Milton said to the consternation of his mom. His dad, changing gears had said nothing. His mom, on the other hand had exploded into a foul mood.

"What!" His mom shouted, nearly dropping her lipstick.

"Why wouldn't you go to confession?" His mom asked, turning to stare at Milton.

"But Mom–"

"No buts, young man. You're a catholic and must adhere to the rules."

"Wait, why am I being picked on? Dad doesn't go either." Milton said, seeing his dad give him the evil eye. His mom turned to stare in shock at her husband. They had just passed the barrier.

"Hold it there, son. What I do is no concern–"

"Really Robert, such a bad example." His mom shook his head. Milton nearly laughed his head off, but kept himself in check. "I can't believe this. We will talk about this when we get home." Mom got back to applying her makeup as if the incident had never happened.

Milton looked through the rear view mirror and saw his dad sliding his index finger across his throat. Milton faked shuddering in terror when their eyes met. Mom cast a confused look at them and shrugged. They both laughed. They had just neared the intersection in the industrial area. The light was green when they crossed over. They had nearly crossed the road when an oil filled tanker shot like a canon ball and slammed into their car. Milton had his seat belt on. For whatever inconceivable reason, his parents had neglected to put on their seat belt that day. The impact knocked his mom sideways into his dad. No one had time to scream. The crunching of metal and the taste of fear was all that Milton felt. The force threw him against the left back door, slamming his left elbow into the glass. The seat belt had lessened the pain. A jarring pain travelled up his arm and ribs. He blacked out and came to again.

"Jesus!" Milton clenched his jaw in a desperate attempt to forget the pain. The car was till being driven towards broken down vehicles on the curb. Sparks were flying all around him. He felt so faint. The car came to a sudden halt. Milton felt a metallic taste in his mouth and spat out blood. Eyes blurry with tears, pain flaring all over his body, he couldn't feel his left arm anymore. *Was it broken*? He glanced to his mom and dad and the scream that rose up in his chest got caught up in his throat. He fainted when he saw their condition.

When he came to, Josh was sitting beside him, tears spilling down his face. Milton met the priest's gaze and instantly felt a kick in his gut. They were gone. He gazed out the hospital window and closed his eyes. A lone tear slid down his face.

FOUR

Milton's parents had died instantly in the car accident or so he was told. A picture of the mangled car had been placed on the front page with the caption MIRACLE BOY SURVIVES HORRIFIC ACCIDENT. For some weeks that had been the sensational news until it wore off and other stories took center stage. Father Grant had skillfully kept Milton and Josh away from the prying eyes of the media. He felt his chest loosening as he expelled the memories. A look around the garage revealed old shoe racks, wooden boxes and old photo frames. Milton picked a frame of his dad with his arm around mum's chest. He smiled wistfully at the pose. He heard their main gate banging and knew Josh was up. He placed the old photo down and picked a dusty burgundy wine bottle. While his dad was not a drunk, he was a frequent connoisseur of vintage wine. Milton spied an old dusty trunk padlocked and approached it. Milton frowned as he brushed away the cobwebs around it. He had never seen it before. He fidgeted with the padlock but could not get it opened. He needed something bigger. He settled on a crowbar. He broke the lock and opened the trunk, sneezing from the smell emanating inside. A bunch of newspaper clippings were inside it. He took them out and spied a red lettered bound book inside the trunk. On it was written, BEWARE THE DARKNESS INSIDE YOU. *Strange*, Milton thought as he tried to open the book. An inner voice warned him not to. He had a premonition that something was off, but couldn't quite determine what. He shrugged it off. He began to unstrap the strange book when he heard shuffling feet behind him. His hand hovered over the half torn strap and stopped.

"Milton." Josh's voice said, dispelling him from doing the deed. He turned around to face Josh. Josh looked rested, but his eyes were still red from shedding tears.

"Father Grant called." Josh said as his eyes switched to the book in his hand.

"What is that?"

"Oh, this, just an old book I saw in dad's stuff." Milton said. Josh nodded and looked around.

"I will be having breakfast at Marian's place." Josh said as he back pedaled. Milton was pleased that he was sobering up.

"Ok. Don't forget to be home early."

"Ok."

Milton stood there, listening to Josh's receding footsteps. He contemplated exploring the book later. He hitched it under his armpit and took the old photo frames. Milton locked the garage and went back inside. He needed to call back the priest. *What could he possibly want with him?* He placed the book under his bed away from Josh' prying eyes. That boy was an avid reader. He picked the landline and made the call.

FIVE

Milton sat in the third pew of St. Mary's parish hall gazing at the statue of Jesus on the wall. After calling back the priest, he had trekked to the church to meet him. The church was empty when he got there. Milton spied a woman entering the confession box so he knew the priest would be with him shortly. His mind drifted as he waited. Milton's gaze was on the Holy Mother cradling the baby Jesus. Bitterness grew in his heart as he thought of the brutal manner in which his parents had died. As a child, he used to love sitting around his mother's feet as she regaled them with stories from the bible. But the joy of adolescence and further reading of biblical stories had left him unsatisfied with its ridiculousness.

"Milton," the voice of the priest emanated from beside him, pulling him out of his thoughts. Milton sat erect as the priest sat beside him.

"How is Josh holding up?" Father Grant asked as he put his hand on his thigh, his cassock trailing on the ground. His weather beaten face smiled kindly at him. Father Grant had been a family friend ever since he came to the town twenty years ago. Milton had heard stories from his dad on how some women had put a bet on who would bed him. Such a man of character. Yet, as Milton side glanced at the priest, he noticed weariness beside that cool façade.

"He will be fine." Milton said, his gaze resting on the altar. On their far right, an old woman sat with her head bowed.

"What about you. Are you ok?" The priest asked, his face took on a more serious demeanor. Milton nodded his head.

"If there is anything you need to talk about, my office is always open." Father Grant said as he stood up. "And I will see you at confession, young man." The priest said, a mock frown on his face. Milton smiled in spite of being found out by the priest. The priest turned around and walked towards the confession booth. Milton found his gaze roaming over the individuals kneeling in the pews. He did not recall the last time he had ever prayed. He felt his stomach rumbling as he walked out of the church hall. It was midday. Milton descended the church's stairs and walked further towards a vendor by the roadside selling Jollof. He stopped by, and bought enough to sate his hunger and moved on.

Milton passed a lot of people who gave him their condolences. He accepted them stoically, but the phrase 'My sympathies' had no meaning for Milton. He had a lot going for him and had no time for false sympathies. Tomorrow he would have to meet the insurance firm and get some explanation as to why the funeral was not covered by them. He decided to take a nap while waiting for Josh to come home. He was asleep even before the thought left his mind.

SIX

M ilton woke up with his heart walloping against his chest. Try as he might, he couldn't remember his dream. It was on the fringe of his mind. Yet he couldn't shake the feeling that there was something he was supposed to remember. His mind was jolted as he heard laughter drifting from the living room. He walked to the window and gazed out. He must have slept for hours. He stood there, pondering what lay ahead for them. He stepped out of his room and entered the kitchen. He poured himself some juice and belched loudly. He wiped his mouth with his left hand, pausing to take in the untidy state the kitchen was in. Unwashed bowls, discarded junk packs lay around. A cleanup had to be done. He sighed as he washed the glass he drank from.

Milton gazed at his handiwork and smiled to himself. He had cleaned the kitchen, as best as he could.

"Loki is so cool." Milton heard Josh's voice drift in from the living room. He had been so busy tidying up, he had forgotten about those two.

"Naah, I would choose black widow any time." Marian replied. Milton smiled when he heard that. Marian, their next door neighbor's daughter, feisty as ever. He entered the living room, plumping down into the sofa. The kids were watching the Avengers, a film about superhumans wearing tight fitting costumes. They were so engrossed in the movie, the two failed to notice his presence. He decided to stoke the fire and he knew what exactly to do.

"Well, I think Hulk is cool." Milton said, casting a wry grin at both of them.

"What!" Both of them said at once. "That green thing?" Josh said, eyes wide like saucers. *Here we go again*, Milton thought. Milton sank into the sofa and waited for the lecture on superheroes Josh was about to give. His able supporter, defender of women, ponytailed Marian nodded her head at his every exposition.

"Come on dude, Loki has these super cool powers..."

SEVEN.

"Shit." Milton spat as he sidestepped a mound of feces beside the road. It was eight in the morning and the town was silent. He had decided to check out the insurance firm. He decided to take a circuitous route to the taxi station, avoiding curious stares from passersby. He didn't have the luxury of accepting fake condolences. Ahead he could hear the baritone voice of the bus conductor as he heralded "Tema station". Milton walked towards a bus with the inscription GOD SAVES. He shook his head at the naivety of some individuals still believing in such mundane notions. While he still believed the universe revolved by the will of the creator, he did not see how such an omnipotent being could bear to see such suffering in the world was something he could never understand. Milton sometimes wondered if the dude, God forgive him for that thought, hadn't taken a sabbatical leave. He entered the rickety bus and sat beside an old man. He waited patiently as the bus filled up. At a quarter past nine, they set from the station. Milton felt his mind straying as the bus chugged its way on the road, emitting a coughing sound as they cruised the road.

"Yes, front please" The young conductor said as he stretched out his palm for their fares. Milton paid his fare, taking care not to touch the dirtied palms of the conductor. He wondered why some bus conductors were unkempt. Would it be too much to ask for a shower in the wee hours of the morning? He alighted in front of the industrial complexes. Milton cursed as the bus blew fumes at him as it trundled away. He shook his head in disbelief. How such a vehicle was still plying the road was a mystery to him?

"Damn!" He sniffed his long sleeved shirt to make sure no fumes were still smelling off him. Milton turned and began to walk towards a whitewashed building. He walked past an ivory sign board and stood at the threshold. SKYLIFE ASSURANCE was written on the bronze door. He pressed the knocker and felt it ringing inside. He heard the patter of heels and waited patiently. He could feel the sweat glistening on his back. He had never felt comfortable wearing formal attire. A doll faced lady dressed in a gray jacket poked her head curiously outside.

"Hello!" The lady said with a warm smile, disarming Milton's apprehensiveness. Milton had always been suspicious of insurers. But looking at the lady he understood why people still signed up for such products despite all the negative reports about it. He guessed it was good business to put a pretty lady up front for the clients to be less suspicious. After all, who wouldn't want to converse with a pretty lady. It made perfect sense to dull your mind while signing your fortune away.

"Hello!" Milton replied back, attempting to deepen his voice.

"Are you Milton?" The lady said with a lopsided grin, but quickly compensated with a cheerful grin. Milton felt his stomach dip. "Yes" He replied, favoring the lady with his cutest smile.

"Please follow me." The lady said as she opened the door for Milton. Gladly, Milton thought as he followed the lady, taking every moment to appreciate the view from the back. He found himself in a brightly lit room. On each side of him were individuals seated behind desk attending to clients. He was shown a door marked CLAIMS ROOM. He was given a seat and waited. The air conditioning made him shiver a bit, and he wished he had brought a jacket. The door closed silently behind him. A grey haired man entered, his belly leading him. He was impeccably dressed in a grey suit. *Rich snob*, Milton thought.

"I am Arthur Agyemang" They shook hands. "I am sorry about your parents." Milton shrugged and nodded.

"I don't mean to be callous, considering the traumatic experience you've been through." The grey haired man said, taking his time to enunciate every word. "We have a bit of an issue with your dad's policy." Milton felt his gut clench. His mouth was dry. This day could not be any worse.

"Go ahead," he said calmly yet his heart was walloping against chest, threatening to burst from his chest.

"Well, the thing is that..."

EIGHT.

In hindsight, Milton should have known that something like that would happen. He had never trusted insurance firms. They always found ways to screw you from behind while smiling at your face, pardon the phrase. He sat on the porch of their house, gazing at the twilight. Josh was still at Marian's place. He had been not been surprised at how calm his younger brother took the news. Case in point, his daddy's account had not been deducted for some time. In effect, they couldn't pay his lump sum. Milton shook his head as he stood and paced the porch. He felt the burden of responsibility heavily on his shoulders. They were now truly alone. How long they would survive on the benefits paid to them from the bank was something he couldn't fathom. He felt a buzz in his pocket and fished out his vibrating phone. Milton glanced at the caller ID. *Who would be calling him at this time?*

He stared at the screen and his heart skipped a beat. It was a voicemail. He listened to it, lips twitching at the corners at the message on it. His dad wouldn't approve of his next step. Milton shrugged, picked his navy blue jacket and walked out of the house, making sure to send Josh a message that he was rendezvousing with Carol.

"IT'S LOUD, RIGHT?" Carol said as they walked through the disco. Overhead, multicolored lights flashed around, casting the place into green, red and yellow ambience. Milton had been overjoyed when the call had come from Carol. He knew he had the hots for her, but also knew it was a bad idea to go out with her. The lights from the dance floor danced across his eyes as they made their way through the gyrating bodies. He avoided everyone's gaze. Barely a week after his parents' death, here he was partying. Some may call it insensitive, he called it living. Milton glanced around to see if he could spot Mark, Carol's boyfriend. News travelled fast. He had heard whispers they were breaking up. Not to sound callous, but a part of him was secretly pleased. He followed Carol to a seat at the far end. Carol was clad in a tight jeans which hugged every curve of her. Milton was trying hard not to stare. A few meters above the crowd, the DJ was busily shuffling music to the cheers of the crowd.

"So what's going on?" Milton asked as they sat down facing each other, a small coffee table was between them. Carol leaned over displaying ample cleavage. Milton took a sharp breath and looked into her eyes. There was a mischievous smile on Carol's lips.

"Mark and I broke up." Carol said matter of factly, stretching to take the coke placed in front of them and taking a sip. Milton found his jaw slacking, but closed it immediately. Many thoughts ran through his mind. Around them the crowd was going crazy with the new hit song playing. His dad was dead and here he was having a good time.

"Are you ok?" Milton asked, meeting her gaze. He was still trying to comprehend why she choose to spill out her hearts in this place. They had been to the same senior high while in school. Milton had always had a crush on her. She knew it no doubt about that. She sometimes teased him about it.

"Yes." Carol said as she leaned her head back, exposing her neckline. Milton felt his heart walloping against his chest. *What was he doing here?* Such thoughts could not be entering his mind. To make matters worse, the DJ put on a slow romantic music. Milton glanced across the dance floor and saw people breaking up into pairs and dancing together.

"Wanna dance?" Carol said, standing up and stretching her right hand towards Milton. Milton hesitated, but saw something in her eyes. *Was it sadness, vulnerability?* He didn't want to disappoint her. A voice screamed in his head, *I can't believe you are doing this to me.* Milton stood up, as Carol put her hands around his shoulders, crushing her chest against his. He reciprocated by putting his hands around her waist. The inner voice screaming at him was silenced as he felt Carol's head upon his shoulders. They danced slowly to the tune of the song.

Milton didn't remember how long they spent on the dance floor. He barely remembered what happened. After much drinking and dancing, butt clinging if you believe it, a friend of Carol dropped him off at his gate. When he got home Josh was asleep. He didn't even bother to undress, but flung himself onto his bed, a smiling tugging at his mouth as he drifted off, every thought of his on the feel of his hands around Carol.

NINE

Milton woke up feeling disoriented and tired. He massaged his temple, a burgeoning headache was throbbing. He wrapped the bedspread around him and got off the bed to stand in front of the mirror. Red eyes stared back at him. Memories of last night flashed in his mind. He winced at some of the things he had done on the dance floor. Oh boy, he couldn't believe the moves he had pulled off on the dance floor.

"So!" Josh announced unceremoniously, ruining his moment. "What did I miss?" He stood at the door, dressed in his pajamas.

"Um, She..." Milton stammered, trying to find the appropriate words to say. "We hung out, that's all." A lifted eyebrow met his stare. Milton felt his face heating up. He couldn't believe he was being quizzed by his little brother.

"Ok. Just remember to use protection next time." Josh said, a smile tugging at his lips.

"We didn't. You little devil," Milton attempted to go after Josh and tripped on the bedspread wrapped around him. Josh backed out of his reach, laughing at his brother's antics.

"Come on, Milton. It's not like we are living in the stone age anymore. They teach these things in school you know."

Milton stared at his brother and said. "Who are you. What have you done with my brother?" Josh only giggled and turned around, whistling to himself. Milton felt relieved his brother was taking everything slow. He was glad.

"So how was the dancing?" Josh's voice sounded from the hallway.

Milton smiled to himself. They were starting the day on a bright note. Breakfast was going to be tough. He sighed. He missed Carol already.

TEN

"This is good," Josh said between mouthfuls. "You've gotten better at cooking ever since you started seeing her."

"Josh!"

"Seriously, dude, I mean, look at this. No wonder you always seem to be slack jawed around her."

"No, I'm not."

"Yes, you are." Josh replied, stuffing an egg into his mouth and munching it.

"You're making things up" Milton said, biting into his sandwich bread and a fried egg.

"Wish I was on the dance floor that day. Dad's ghost would have fainted upon seeing you dancing." The mention of their dad brought a lull in the conversation.

"I miss them you know." Milton said. They were seated opposite each other in the living room. The clock on the wall, a gift from their grandfather chimed nine in the morning.

"Me too." Josh said, casting his eyes downwards for a moment. They were both quiet for some time, each lost in his own thoughts Milton was surprised at how resilient Josh had been throughout the funeral.

"Are you gonna be ok... in school tomorrow?" Milton asked, draining his cup of tea. He wiped his mouth with the back of his hand. A habit his mother had always chided him for.

Josh chewed his egg thoughtfully as he formed a reply. "Yeah." He shrugged. "What could possibly go wrong?"

For a young boy, Josh was intelligent and intuitive. Milton guessed that's why their parents' death hadn't had a drastic toll yet. Josh reminded him so much of their father. He remembered with fondness, the little pep talks he always had with him and Josh.

"What about you. Are you going to get a new job?" Josh asked as he came round to Milton's side, scooping up the utensils to rinse them.

"Still searching. The priest said he had news for me. Will meet him this afternoon to discuss my prospects."

"Ok. That's good news. At least we will get some variety here." Josh shouted from the kitchen. "I almost forgot," Josh poked his head at the door. "Marian's parents would be going to the mall. Um, can I tag along?" Josh said with a pleading look in his eyes.

Milton feigned contemplating about it. "Ok. But don't stay too long."

"Yes!" He hollered. "So can I leave now?" Josh asked, grinning misheviously at Milton.

"Not in that." Milton admonished. Josh glanced at his pajamas and grinned sheepishly.

"Oh, this. I completely forgot. Um, my stuff is at Marians place."

"Ohk. We need to have a serious chat when you get back." Milton said with a mocking tone.

"Ok, mom."

"You–"

Josh sped out of the door before Milton could retort. Milton turned when he heard the door creaking. To his surprise Josh poked her head at the door and said. "Will she come here?" Josh asked, Milton faced registered confusion. Then the truth dawned on him.

"Josh!" But he was already gone. He wondered what they were teaching them in school. He needed to make haste and go meet the priest.

MILTON FOUND HIMSELF sweating as he sat in Father Grant's study. He despised long sleeved shirts. He loved his lacoste and jeans. His mom's distaste for that had always amused him. She had scolded him once when he had worn jeans to church. He remembered the look on her face when he had replied God would be okay with his dressing so long as his heart was right with Him. Well, it hadn't gone as well as he had thought. A lecture on a dressing holier than thou had struck home the message. He smiled wryly at such memories. The picture of the holy mother on the wall, cradling baby Jesus reminded him of the "hail Mary's" they had recited together every morning. He felt footsteps behind him and quickly composed himself. Father Grant entered the study carrying a thick volume of God knows what.

"Hello Milton! How are you this morning?" He said as he took a seat across the desk from him. He placed the volume on an even bigger stack of books. Around the room, books were stacked on shelves. He even saw Dan Brown's Da vinci Code. *Interesting*, he thought. He never pegged the priest as one to read such books.

"I have seen better days, Father." Milton replied, shifting his eyes from the shelves.

"I see you were perusing my shelf. Surprised by some of the collections, eh?"

"I was—"

"Maybe one day I will tell you why. But first things first." He said, opening a drawer and pulling a brown envelope from inside. "About your job, I got in touch with a colleague of mine and he has agreed to meet you on Monday. He leaned back and clasped his hand. "I forwarded a copy of your CV to him"

"Thank you, Father." Milton said, smiling back at the priest.

The priest waved him away. "That's one of the few favors I can do for your family. Besides, that's not the main reason why I called you here."

Milton felt his gut churning. *What could the priest be talking about?* He hoped to God it wasn't about the dancing thing.

"Your dad expressed the fear that you were losing your faith, Milton." The priest said, staring at Milton in a grim but non condescending manner.

"Really, he said that?" He replied, lost for words. The priest tapped the desk gently with his forefinger. Father Grant waited patiently for him to continue. When none was forthcoming, he went on.

"It's not a bad thing to doubt yourself, Milton. We are only human, yearning to understand how the world works. Sometimes to believe, you must battle your inner demons." He leaned his elbows on the desk. " The Lord reveals himself to each of us in his own way."

"Did God reveal himself to you, Father?" Milton asked. The priest smiled at his question. "That is a story I would love to share with you, regrettably not today." *Priests, always with veiled answers*, Milton thought.

"What if he was right? I mean what if I am losing my faith?"

"Then I guess you must look deep within yourself and ask the question: Is there anything else apart from this physical life?"

The words of the priest struck a chord deep within him. Milton was lost in thought for a few minutes. Father Grant stood up from his seat and came round to sit on the edge of the desk. Milton could smell the tinge of incense on the priest.

"I know you're bitter now. But in time you'll understand. Some things happen for a reason."

Milton snorted. "I'm sorry I don't want to sound rude, but– "

"I know, son." Father Grant said, putting his right hand on his shoulder."Someday you will understand, of that I am certain."

ELEVEN

After leaving Father Grant's study, Milton contemplated buying a new shirt for his interview. He saw a kiosk and approached it. He loaded credit onto his smartphone and walked off. He had to take a left turn to branch into his main street but decided to take a shorter route through tightly packed buildings. People built with no sense of style. He had just branched into a lane filled with puddle when a body slammed into him. Swearing, he untangled himself and faced his assailant.

"Mark, what are you– " He crouched low, ducking a swing from Mark. Milton grabbed Mark's waist and flung him into a wall, pinning his left behind him. Mark stank of alcohol.

"What the hell, Mark?" He tried to tighten his grip, but Mark twisted out of his grip.

"Stay away from Carol. She is mine."

"What are you talking about? " Milton said, spying a crowd gathering. This day was getting weirder and weirder. People now had something to gossip about.

"Stay away from her." Mark said as he backed away. The crowd began to disperse, whispering in hushed tones.

"Damn it." Milton cursed. Just when he thought things were going right. He saw an eye of a face in a window giving him a strange look. He cast his eyes down to avoid any strange stares from people as he approached his house. News travelled fast in this town. He immediately went into the shower and stared at his face. A rendition of Taylor Swift's 'you will remember' began to play in the living room. He stepped out from the shower, a white towel around his waist. He smiled as he picked the call.

"Hello Carol!" Milton said, a wide grin on his face.

"Hey, I heard what happened. Are you okay?"

"Yeah. It was nothing. Just boys being boys."

"It's my fault. I shouldn't have–"

"You're not to blame for anything." Milton cut her off. "You shouldn't feel sorry."

" So when are you going for the interview." Carol asked.

"How did you?" Milton paused. "Never mind, I know who told you." Milton put the phone between his nook of his left shoulder and left ear as he smeared pomade on his hands.

"Ah, you want to hear the juicy details, huh?" Milton said as he grinned from ear to ear.

Milton knew it wasn't right. He should wait for some time, but he didn't want to lose this chance to be with the one girl he had pined for all these years. He put on a jeans short and sat on his bed, bare chested. He contemplated what to do next and remembered the red book he had picked from the garage. He tore the red strip binding it and opened it. A huge thunderclap boomed outside, startling him, but he shrugged it off to the rainy season they were in. The first page was blank. Milton flipped through blank pages with a confused frown. *What book is this?* He almost shoved the book away when he saw a page with some runic writings on it. They were written in tiny curls of writings. He brought the book closer to his face and read.

"Dear reader, if you are reading this book, then you have stumbled upon one of the greatest treasures and the curses of the past. The knowledge hidden from the world is at your fingertips. Continue at your own peril."

Milton paused, brow furrowing. *Why would his dad have a book like this?* He read the last note.

"DARE TO READ IF YOU CAN!"

Milton felt his heart walloping against his chest. Now such a book would make a best seller. He began to flip through the pages again and frowned. He gasped at drawings of various demons and angels. Several incantations were scribbled beneath the drawings. The diagrams and pentagrams reminded him of the seventh and eight books of Moses. It was a banned book, but thanks to the internet he had read a fair share of it. Yet this book went even further, expounding in great detail the origins and rituals to summon such creatures. He had read and heard tales of exoteric rituals to summon beings like that, but he had never paid any heed to such stories. Pure fiction, he called them.

"Is this the real deal?"

He flipped further, heart pounding at each new revelation. He paused at a page with a drawing of a tombstone with a figure in a cowl standing over it. Its gnarled fingers curled around a staff. Summoning the spirit of the dead. Milton wiped his right hand across his brow. The fan was on yet he felt hot. Dread and hope were churning inside him.

What if he could speak to mom and dad? He had never gotten the chance to say goodbye. He banished such thoughts from his mind. The living had no place communing with the dead. The footnote revealed something interesting. The author stated in the footnotes that Saul had used such an incantation to raise Samuel's spirit from the dead. Milton was familiar with the biblical story of King Saul. While he had enjoyed reading the stories of the bible, he didn't really believe all the stories were real. Yet he debated the merits of this unknown author giving credence to such stories.

Milton flipped into to another page. The title caught his attention: SUMMONING DEMONS TO DO YOUR BIDDING. Now that is interesting. He read on, pausing intermittently to digest what the author meant.

These demons when properly summoned can do any bidding within their power. From their ability to heal, grant wishes. These were the most sought after in the ancient days. Notable among them was..

Milton chewed his lips as he glanced through the list of names. He particularly liked the last one. He hesitated mentioning it. He couldn't believe the book was getting to him. *Creepy*. He flipped to the last page and saw a cautionary note from the author.

Never summon a demon when you do not have anything to offer in return. You have been warned.

Milton closed the book with a clap. It's just pure fiction, he said to himself. *What if it was true?* He opened the book again and read the authors final words.

"Hey!"

He leaped off the bed amidst Josh's laughter. Heart pounding and flushed with embarrassment as he wagged his finger at Josh.

"You nearly gave me a heart attack, man."

"Wow!. You were zoned out there, man. Lost entirely in the book." The red book lay between them. Josh picked it up and threw it to Milton. "Maybe I will read it when you are done. What's it about anyway?" Josh asked, unbuttoning his shirt and stepping out of his shoes.

"Some gibberish about the myths of the ancient world."

"Sounds fun. Anything to eat?" Josh said he walked out, presumably towards the kitchen.

That was close. Milton stared at the clock. It was nearly dusk outside. He must have been reading for a long time. He threw the book on the bed, covering it with his pillow.

"Later buddy."

TWELVE

Milton woke feeling terrible. Strange, he couldn't remember any of his dreams. He groaned as he dragged himself from his bed and approached the mirror. Red eyes stared back at him.. He heard movements in the living room and went to check. Josh in a white shirt with matching black pants was whistling while packing his textbooks into his bag. Josh stopped whistling when he saw Milton standing, grinning at him.

"Good morning. What's up with you. You were talking in your sleep last night."

Milton frowned, obviously surprised he would be talking in his dreams. "What was I saying?"

"Some gibberish about demons, I think. That book must be intense." Josh said as he flung his backpack over his shoulder and walked towards the main door.

"Hey, don't get into trouble at school." Milton said, earning a grin from Josh.

"Whenever have I ever been mischievous?" Milton only rolled his eyes. He watched the door close slowly behind Josh.

"So what do we do now." He said to no one in particular.

MILTON PEERED AT THE image on his laptop. He was researching materials he would need for his interview. He lazily surfed his way through the tons of information on the screen. After Josh had left, he had done a bit of tidying up around the house. He recalled how every

Wednesday, their mom would wake them up in the morning for devotion. He hated it, yet always acquiesced to her demands. He remembered the many frustrations he had put his mother through. Milton winced at the memories. *What he wouldn't do to have them back?* An odd thought surfaced in his mind, but he waved it off. His attention was drawn to a news article on the spate of the economy. The freeze on employment was still on. He shook his head. How many such policies were saving the government money yet depriving the very people they were serving of their livelihood. He spent some time reading on interviewing techniques and FAQS.

Milton yawned and glanced at his phone. It was nearly midday. He couldn't believe it. He had been reading aimlessly for nearly three hours. The phone beside his laptop began to buzz. He frowned. *Who would be calling him at this time?* He despised picking unknown calls. You never know when someone was trying to prank you. He hesitated for a minute, but eventually picked it up.

"Hello!" A voice on the other line said.

" Yes, I'm Milton." He answered to a question that was asked.

"He what!" Milton felt his mouth dry up as he listened to the speaker on the other line. When the call ended, he stood there, hands trembling, unable to process what had just happened. In his mind, all he could scream was God don't let this happen. He closed the lid of his laptop and rushed out of the door almost forgetting to lock it.

THIRTEEN.

The Metropolitan Hospital's corridors were crowded with a gamut of individuals as Milton waded through. The waft of chlorine greeted anyone that entered its interior. Pregnant women lay on the benches waiting for their turn at the OPD. Angry and pale looking faces with yellowish eyes gazed at you as you bypassed them. Milton never saw any of these as he rushed through the people. He nearly collided with a disabled being trundled in a wheel chair. He veered into a narrow corridor, and paused, gasping for breath from all the running. He poked his head into a room.

"Hey!"

"Sorry!" Milton said as he backtracked from a red faced nurse. He had just witnessed a naked butt being injected with a syringe. He could picture the look of dismay on the patient's face. He run from that section with the backdrop of the nurse's cajoling. A few metres away from him, he spied a door marked CASUALTY and entered, not bothering to knock. He was immediately blocked by a burly female attendant.

"What do you want here?" The woman said, frowning at him. Milton paused, thinking about the response to give, one that wouldn't get him booted out.

"Um, sorry. I'm Milton Freeman. I got a call from someone here that my little brother had been admitted here." Milton said as he wiped the sweat from his brow. He felt the slickness of his own sweat at his back. The attendant's gaze softened when she heard that.

"Josh Freeman?" She said as her face drooped in pity. "Walk down the corridor and ask for the critical room." Milton felt his gut churning with anxiety. He managed to nod and turned back, noticing for the first time the numerous patients lying on beds in the room. He did as the attendant asked and came to the door as described but hesitated to proceed. He knocked this time and waited. When no response was forthcoming, he opened the door, revealing a small bed with a beeping machine at the bed's edge. He padded towards the bed and saw a figure with an oxygen mask on. His head was bandaged. Milton had felt despair at his parent's death, but staring at the body of his brother on the bed, his spirit was crushed.

Oh God! How did this happen? Milton wondered to himself. *Was his family cursed*? A single tear run down his face. He wiped it with his left hand. Josh, larger than life, who had been the thorn in his side, yet he couldn't bear to lose his brother. He heard footsteps approaching and swiftly composed himself. He went to stand beside the bed facing the door. A grey haired man holding a pad in his left hand entered. From the overall he wore, Milton surmised he was the doctor. The man paused, sizing up Milton. His glance passed from Milton to Josh, a grim smile on his face.

"I presume you're Milton. A nurse spoke to you earlier on the phone. I'm Doctor Raymond." He extended his hand towards Milton. Milton reciprocated and shook his hand in a firm grip.

"Did you see any nurse in here?" The doctor asked as he came round to Josh's side.

"No" Milton said, surprised by the question. The doctor shook his head. He moved closer to Josh side, and squinted at the beeping monitor overhead.

"How is he, Doctor?" Milton asked.

"For now, his condition is stable, but we will keep monitoring." The doctor replied curtly as he scribbled down something on his pad.

"Is there um– "

"I'll not give you false hope. Your brother suffered a serious blow to his head from the fall. At this point we will do our best to keep monitoring him. Yours is to be there for him." The doctor said leveling his gaze at Milton. The doctor did something uncharacteristic. He patted Milton on the shoulder. Milton nodded, choking back the tears. The room was silent when the doctor went out. The steady beep of the monitor was the only sound in the room. The rhythmic breathing of Josh through the mask made Josh cringe every time he heard it. He hoped Josh wasn't suffering. They had probably shot him with a few doses of morphine to lessen the pain.

Someone knocked on the door, knocking him out of his brooding. Through the window he could see the sunset. He asked the individual to enter. The priest entered, nodding at him as he glanced at Josh.

"I came as soon as I heard. What are the doctor's saying?"

"Not much. But they say he is stable."

"You must stay strong, Milton." Father Grant said as he clasped his hands together.

Milton felt a surge of anger and turned to stare at Josh. He didn't want the priest to see the anger on his face. He took a deep breath to calm his nerves. It would be unwise to talk back at the priest. He decided to patronize him even though he felt disdain for the words of the priest. Outside, the sun had turned to a dull red in the sky. In the distance, he could hear the call of the muezzin.

FOURTEEN

Milton sat with Josh as the hours passed by. The priest kept him company but had to leave around six pm for church activities. Milton heard the priest say something about organizing a prayer meeting. He mumbled his thanks, just to be polite. He sat on a wobbly chair beside Josh and willed him to get better. *How he wished those positive thinking mantras would work right now*. The nurses came and went, but Josh remained still only his chest indicating any sign of life. He felt hunger gnawing at his stomach yet decided to hold on further.

Carol came by later in the night after her shift at the hotel where she worked ended. She attempted to cheer him up by sitting beside him and giving him words of encouragement. She had to leave for home since she would be leaving early for work. She promised to call him after work. Milton was even more surprised when Mark came around. At first, Milton was apprehensive. He wasn't sure what to make of his appearance. He found his uneasiness misplaced when Mark apologized for the brawl they had. They both laughed off the incident good naturedly. Mark asked about Josh's health. He stayed for a few minutes and left. As Milton watched Mark walking way, he couldn't help but think how amusing it was that his brother had to be hurt for them to settle their differences.

Around eleven, a night attendant came around. One look at Milton, and she scowled at him and admonished him to get something to eat. He wouldn't be any use if he was dead. She promised to watch over him like her own son. Hunger made him so weak. He slipped out of the hospital and felt the cold chill of the night. He spied people sitting on the pavements, some snoring, others waiting for their families. The waiting was the hardest. Not knowing what would happen. He rummaged through his pockets and offered a twenty to a roadside vendor. He took a can coke and some biscuits. He crunched the biscuits and went back inside. The television in the OPD was showing a local movie, but he was too preoccupied to watch. He saw a few patients glued to the screen. His thoughts turned to how unpredictable his life was turning out to be. His parents and now his brother. He drained the coke before entering the room where Josh was. With the exception of the TV, the whole hospital was like a cemetery. His bladder felt full. He searched for a urinal and found one, locking himself in it. He sat on the closet and sighed, releasing his bladder. His shoulders felt numb. In the quietness of the closet, Milton did something he had failed to do in a long time. He prayed.

Milton went back to Josh's side. He sat by his side and stared at the monitor above Josh's head. Outside, he could hear the faint blaring of a discotheque in town. He felt his eyelids dropping and the last thought on his mind was probably the devil having a laugh at their predicament.

FIFTEEN

THUMP! THUMP! Milton was running in a semi light tunnel. His skin was prickling at the noise coming from behind him. It was a dream that much he knew. Scrawny hands protruded from the walls of the tunnel. Each was trying to grab onto him. A maniacal laughter reverberated across the tunnel. Every hair on his head was on edge. A rhythmic pounding was gaining slowly on him.

"YOU ARE MINE, BOY!"

Milton woke up drenched in sweat. For a moment, he looked lost in the room he was in. The dream was rapidly languishing from his consciousness. He yawned and cast his eyes around, settling on Josh. Reality hit him and he felt dread in his heart. There was no movement, only the rise and fall of Josh's chest. The beeping monitor showed no improvements. A streak of light doused the wall from a slit in the blinds. He used his shirt to wipe his face, making sure to wipe off any drool from his face. He did not have long to wait. The doctor entered, trailed by a nurse, a trainee it seemed.

"Good morning Milton." The doctor said as he entered. Milton mumbled a reply and moved aside as he came to Josh's side. "I see you've been up all night." The doctor checked Josh's pulse and whispered something to the nurse who nodded. Milton looked on, amazed at the efficiency of the doctor. He bit back his tongue to ask how Josh was. By the grim look on the doctor's face, he knew it wasn't good. The doctor placed back the stethoscope around his neck and slipped off his glasses.. He looked at Milton squarely in the eye.

"Your brother's condition hasn't changed." The doctor said as the nurse looked on sadly. "We might need him moved to a specialist hospital."

Milton felt the last glimmer of hope dying out. "Move him?"

"Yes. He needs to have a specialist doctor take a second look at him." The doctor said gently, wiping at his eye. Meanwhile, the nurse attempted to look inconspicuous. Milton didn't blame her.

"This hospital is not equipped to deal with his condition."

"And how will we afford the bills. Our insurance cover will not afford the bill over there. Is there something that can be done?" Milton pleaded, looking searchingly at the doctor. The doctor paused, closed his eyes for a moment.

"We will see what we can do. In the meantime, we will make arrangements for him to be moved to the military hospital tomorrow to prevent his condition from deteriorating." The doctor said in a toneless voice. Milton imagined the good doctor had dealt with numerous cases like this. He didn't blame him. Milton gazed at the reading on the monitor, willing it to change. Out of his peripheral vision, he saw the doctor and his sidekick walking out. He saw several missed calls from Carol. It was 8:00 AM. He felt the despair crawling in his heart. Short of a miracle, he knew nothing that could bring his brother back. He began to pace around the room hands on his head. He was startled when a different nurse came in. Looking at the things in her hand, Milton surmised Josh was about to be washed down. He needed to go home and freshen up.

AFTER TAKING HIS BATH, he passed by a familiar joint and silenced his rumbling stomach with some hot porridge. He made his way back towards the hospital. On his way, he met a few people who asked about Josh. He tried to sound nonchalant as he could to anyone who queried him about Josh.

Milton wanted to kill time and get his mind in the right place so he used the main road. As he walked beside the road, he saw a madman picking litter and stocking them up in his burly sack on his back. Milton shook his head at such absurdity. Sane humans littered the street and the insane cleaned it. The sight of the madman brought an incident to mind which brought a smile to his face. Once, his mom had spoken of a bizarre incident that had happened at a wedding ceremony. The bride in her glittering flowery gown stood at the altar under the droning voice of the officiating priest. The minister had just given the go ahead for the groom to kiss the bride. Out of nowhere, busted this madman, grabbed the bride and planted a full kiss on her lips. The whole church was stunned. The madman fled before he could be apprehended. As for the bride, she fainted. It must have been horrifying for her. Milton started guffawing when he recalled that story. Passersby gazed at him quizzically. He finally made it to the hospital in a good mood. He had spent two hours at home. He heard singing as he neared the room that Josh was in. He frowned as he turned his knob and peered through the slit. A circle of church members were around Josh's bed. Milton silently closed the door and waited. He sat on a bench and rested his elbows on his thighs.

Milton understood the need to pray yet a part of him rebelled against that notion. *What could prayer accomplish?* His mom had been an ardent Christian, waking up at dawn to pray, yet she died in a bloody and freaking accident. *Where was God, huh?* He felt his heart beat rising when a hand tapped his shoulder.

"Hey, why didn't you come in?" Father Grant said, looking down at Milton.

"I, Um. Didn't want to intrude."

"Don't push yourself too hard, Milton. Sometimes you need to have faith things will be alright" *Yeah, like mom and dad,* Milton thought. Milton nodded, glancing at the member's filing out of the room. He saw a few people he knew, but he was not acquainted with them.

"I guess I must hope for the best." Milton said, favoring the priest with a wry smile. The priest smiled back. "Way to go, son."

"I have talked to the church. We would do some contribution to help–"

"I really can't–"

"I'm not accepting no for an answer, young man." Father Grant said sternly while his face managed to hold a dint of a smile.

Milton thanked the priest and accepted a few kind words from the rest of the group. He went in the room, noticing that Josh's dressing had been changed. He was still in a catatonic state. He saw a magazine on a table beside Josh and took it. He sat beside his brother, recalling their childhood together. Milton remembered how Josh loved to listen to the story of the elves and the shoemaker. He missed those times. Now gazing at his brother, he feared he was losing him. Looking at Josh, there wasn't any hospital in Ghana equipped to handle such a case. Case in point, Josh wasn't going to last long. It was a bleak outlook. Around mid afternoon, the doctor came to see Milton. He gave Milton the full dose of the situation.

Frankly, after the doctor left, he thought both ideas the doctor put out were bullshit. Either take him to a specialist hospital for an experimental treatment or hope for the best with the current treatment. He went out of the room to clear his head. The beeping sounds made it difficult for him to think. He stood in the corridor, Josh's room at his back.

"Excuse me." A nurse said, wheeling a man with a gaping wound on his right leg. A wide gash was on his eyebrow. Milton grimaced. The world was a cruel place. The faint odor of antiseptic and chlorine was still around. A vivid image of Josh's marker popped into his mind. HERE LIES A LOVELY BROTHER AND SON. Milton winced, dispelling the image from his mind. *Had he given up hope already?*

He once again went to Josh's side and grabbed his hand. "I'm not going to let you die, brother." Milton said as a lone tear fell on Josh's hand. Through the window, the sun was dimming. It was nearly dusk. He felt hunger pangs. "I would sell my soul to the devil himself to bring you back." Milton reiterated as a cold realization dawned on him. Goose pimples prickled all over him. He would do anything for his brother. As those infamous words kept replaying in his mind, he knew how ludicrous it sounded but what if it was possible. As these thoughts coalesced into one single answer, he heard the first patter of rains on the roof.

"I will save you, brother," he whispered as he closed the door behind him, shutting out the unbearable beeping sound. "Even if I have to make a deal with the devil."

SIXTEEN

Milton's sandals squelched as he waded through the deluge that beat him mercilessly. Lightning streaked across the dark skies, illuminating the world in a swirl of colors. He was dripping wet and shivering when he made it home. He groped his way across the hall and switched on the main switch. Outside, thunder boomed, rattling the doors and causing his heart to thud in his chest. He padded his way towards his room, every step dripping water onto the tiled floor. He had to tread carefully to avoiding slipping. His door creaked as he opened it. Milton switched on the light in his room. He sat on his bed, head in his palm. The burden of what he was about to do weighed heavily on his mind. The supernatural was something he had always scoffed at. He pulled out the red book from under his bed being careful not to wet it with his hand. He placed it beside him and grabbed his bedspread and cleaned himself. He glanced up at the holy cross on the wall. Outside, the rains still continued.

Milton picked up the red book, every part part of him screaming for him to stop this madness. He flipped to the page on healing and gazed intently at the sigil of the demon he had to conjure. His heart was thudding in his chest. His ear was bombarded with the sounds of his beating heart. His mouth was dry and he felt hot, despite the chilly atmosphere. Sweat trickled down his brow. He wiped his brow with his left hand and proceeded to read how to summon the demon of healing. Every part of him rebelled at what he was about to do. *He simply had no choice or did he?* His parents, and now Josh. He began to read about the attributes of the demon, focusing on the correct method of summoning a demon. He paused when he reached the text of offering something in return. It was nearly midnight when he finally read through the instructions. He was careful to memorise all salient bits to his mind. *What was he willing to offer in return? Was he really ready to give up his soul? Would his soul be damned forever?*

Milton stood up and took a chalk from his dressing cabinet. He moved away his floor mat and drew the sigil of the demon, careful to draw it as the book prescribed. Through his window, flashes of lightning still streaked across the dark skies. It was almost as if nature had conspired to make the night as frightening as it could possibly be. The sigil faced directly in front of his dressing mirror. He avoided staring at himself in the mirror. He sat crossed legged before the sigil, the red book in his lap. He lit a candle and placed it the middle of the sigil. His heart thudding in his chest, he flipped to the page of summoning. His gut churned. He paused on the summoning page and closed his eyes. He gathered his resolve. He thought of his brother and clenched the knife beside him. A gift from his father on his tenth birthday. He clenched his teeth as he slid the knife across his palm and let the crimson blood drip onto the sigil. As the book had commanded, he began to chant the name of the demon. Outside, the rain had stopped. The night was silent. Milton noticed none of these things. His mind was bent on only one task. The thought of his brother dying was too much for him. He continued to chant, every part of him tingling with an unknown awareness. He put his bloodied hands in the middle of the sigil and uttered the words of summoning.

"I SUMMON YOU DEMON BUER!"

THE ONLY SOUND MILTON could hear was the thumping of his heart in his chest. Not a sound could be heard. The rain had stopped. Despair began to creep into his heart as tears shimmered in his eyes. He had failed his brother. He picked the book and flung it the mirror.

Milton glanced at the bloody line in his left palm. *What had he been thinking*? He heard the door creaking and glanced sideways. He remembered locking the door. It stood ajar.. He closed it and heard the loud chime of the wall clock in the hall. It was exactly midnight.

Milton gasped when the lights went out suddenly. He gripped the door handle tightly. *What was going on?*

Then he heard the footsteps in the hall.

"Who is there?" He shouted, heart pounding in his ears.

BANG!

The door banging caused him to gasp in fright. The lights came on suddenly. He heard something scuttling across the roof.

"Oh God forgive me. What have I done?" He whispered as sweat run down his face.

"ENOUGH!" He bellowed, not out of bravery but fear. The noise stopped at once. Not even the sound of chirping crickets could be heard. He exhaled slowly. Maybe he had an overactive imagination. Something flickered in his peripheral vision. He got closer to the dressing mirror. Then he heard the laughter. At first, he thought his ear was deceiving him. It was emanating from all around him. Eyes wide, he glanced around, his heart was walloping in his chest. It was a wonder he hadn't fainted from terror.

THUMP!

Milton jumped, nearly dislocating his foot when he landed. A scream stuck in his throat. He heard a crack and turned to glance at the mirror. He wiped the sweat getting into his eyes. A thin crack began to appear in the mirror, trailing its way down. Milton got closer, heart pounding. Then he saw the red eyes staring at him from the mirror and screamed. He turned around sideways and saw nothing. Hands on his chest, he began to hyperventilate. He back tracked and felt himself slip on the blood on the floor. Pain flared around his head as he hit the floor. The last thing Milton heard before he blacked out was a guttural laugh in the room. Then everything went dark.

SEVENTEEN.

Milton woke up with a gasp. He was lying on his back, temple throbbing from the burgeoning headache. The sun filtered through the drapes bathing the room in a golden swirl of colors. He rubbed his temple with his right hand and gazed at the bulb in his room still on. The lights were never on when he slept. Then he remembered, his back aching as he stood up. The pain in his left hand, causing him to wince. A red welt had spread in his palm. He had to get that checked before it got infected. Milton gazed at the mirror, spying the red book lying in front of it. The mirror wasn't cracked. He frowned, puzzled at the spectacle before him. He clearly remembered throwing the book at the mirror. He closely examined the surface of the mirror and saw no evidence of a crack. *Had it been a dream?* He stretched forth his hand to pick the red book when he heard the front door bell ringing. He paused, startled by the intrusion.

Milton wiped his face with a discarded cloth and went to get the door. He breathed a sigh of relief when he saw that it was his next-door neighbor. He plastered a wry smile on his face and opened the door, hiding his injured hand behind him.

"Good morning." Milton greeted, wondering what Albert was doing here early in the morning.

"Morning." Albert responded, appraising Milton before continuing. "I saw your front gate opened and just checked to be sure everything was alright." Albert said, pointing at the gate.

Milton must have forgotten to lock the gate yesterday in a desperate bid to embark on his foolhardy plan. He smiled sheepishly, scratching his head for something to say.

"Ooh. I... must have forgotten."

"Oh. Ok. Careful though. With last night outages and all. One can never be too careful" Albert said, glancing at his Rolex.

Milton's ears perked up when he heard about the outages. He hoped it wasn't because of what happened last night.

"Ok. Thanks." Milton said, trying to look composed when in fact inside him his emotions were roiling. Albert simply nodded and backtracked, side stepping a puddle. He stared at the retreating figure of his neighbor. He had been surprised at his action. They hadn't been really close. Just an occasional hello had been what transpired between them. He wondered what had changed that as he closed the door. He walked into the hall and his gaze fell on the wall clock.

"Bollocks!"

He had overslept. Today was the day Josh was being moved. He couldn't believe it. He had to be at the hospital to sign certain documents. He dashed to the bathroom, careful not to open up the cut across his palm. He was putting on a new lacoste when his gaze fell on the red book. He paused, mixed emotions on his face. He took it and flung it under the bed. He picked his phone and powered it on. He scrolled through the messages and frowned when he saw an unknown number. He dialed it listened to the recorded message. Milton stiffened when he heard the message. This couldn't be. Heart walloping against his chest, he sprinted towards the taxi station.

TAXI!

Milton screamed at a cab passing by him not caring how weird he appeared in the wee hours of the morning.

"Where to boss?" The driver with a toothy grin asked.

"To the hospital." Milton said, responding in kind with a wide grin on his face. At last something good had arrived.

MILTON CALMED HIS BEATING heart as he neared the hospital where Josh was in intensive care. The rush of exhilaration he felt when he had answered the strange call had diminished. *What if it was a hoax*? He bypassed a cross section of patients at the OPD and branched into the corridor that led to Josh's room. He halted when he saw the priest and the doctor engaged in an animated conversation. He heard snippets of a "miracle" and "impossible". They both paused when he approached them. The priest beamed him a smile.

"Hello Milton!" The priest said, extending his right arm towards Milton. He shook the priest's arm, nodding to the doctor as well.

"Well, I was called to come to the hospital. I have some good news I believe." Milton said, glancing from the doctor to the priest.

"Certainly. See for yourself." The doctor pointed at Josh's room, a warm smile on his face. Father Grant urged him on. Milton took a deep breath and padded towards the door, he opened it slowly and paused at the entrance, too stunned to speak. He blinked, wishing that what he was seeing was not an illusion.

"Yo, big bro," the familiar, witty voice of Josh filled the room. Milton felt a heaviness in his chest give way. His lips curled into a smile. He blinked the tears that appeared in his eyes. No need to let Josh make a fuss of his tears. A nurse was helping him into his shirt.

"So you do not even wait for one minute and you are trying to woo this beautiful nurse." Milton said, giving the nurse blushing from his comment a mischievous wink. She shook her head at the silliness of the two brothers. She packed her stuff and left the room. Both brothers watched her go. He turned his eyes to see Josh staring at him smugly.

"What now?"

"You were checking her out, weren't you?"

"I don't know what you're talking about." Milton said he plopped beside Josh on the bed. He poked Josh in the ribs.

"So what am I missing? How did this happen.?"

Josh shrugged. "I can't explain. One minute I am at the door of death, one moment I am here waiting to eat my favorite food. I am famished. Got anything to eat." Josh, as cavalier as always.

"You sure everything is alright." Milton poked him him the chest. Josh only giggled and backed away from him. Milton was glad Josh was well. Yet something didn't feel right.

"Well, at least we should thank God that you're alive even if you left half your brain behind." They both laughed. Milton heard voices outside and peeked through the window.

"What is it?" Josh asked from behind him, apprehension in his voice. They said bad news travelled fast. Well, nothing travelled fast like amateur reporters in search of a story.

"We have got to get you out of here before they turn you into a local celebrity." Milton said, a glint in his eye.

"You betcha!"

"Let's do it."

"WE FOOLED THOSE REPORTERS, right?" Milton said as he slumped into the sofa. Josh grinned and opened the fridge, popped a can coke.

"Are you sure that's a good idea.?" Milton asked, nodding towards the can in his hand. Josh answered by draining almost half of the can and giving a loud burp. Milton shook his head at his brother's antics. It was good to have his brother back.

"Did you miss me, bro?"

"Nope."

"Figured as much."

"Were you in pain the whole time.?" Milton asked, gazing intently at Josh. Josh took a seat opposite him, he sipped the can coke before responding. "Not really. They must have put me on some drugs. The doctor said it was miraculous. Maybe God did finally hear those prayers of yours."

"Maybe." Milton responded, gazing up at the ceiling. A nagging sensation was creeping up his spine. *What if yesterday's rituals had worked? What have I done?*

"You okay, bro?" Josh said, staring at Milton with the can halfway to his lips. Milton only smiled, getting up from the sofa.

"You'll be attending the prayer meeting, right? The priest said something about that."

Milton paused. He had nearly forgotten about the Friday prayer meeting, which had been announced in church. It was dusk. They had a few hours to beat before leaving.

"But Josh, you just came back. Don't you think you should rest?"

"Yeah, I know, but having heard all the night vigils you guys had kept for me. I might as well go in person so that I can thank them." Milton shook his head. Using that logic, there was no way he could avoid the programme. Milton squinted at Josh.

"Who are you? What have you done with my brother?"

"I had a near death experience. That sort of thing changes you." Josh said, as he rolled his eyes at Milton.

"Pfft!" Milton harumped and shook his head. "Says the one who never liked alnight service."

"Hey, time changes, bro."

"Whatever. Wake me up when it's time." Milton said as he reclined back into the sofa. He hoped his dreams would be peaceful this time.

EIGHTEEN.

M ilton woke up disturbed by the dream he had. He tried to grasp onto the dream but felt it slipping front his grasp. He felt a cold chill tingling down his spine. Something was coming. Dread filled his heart. He felt a foreboding. He heard the wall clock chiming but felt too sluggish. He fished in his pocket and took out his phone. What if he called the priest and confessed to him everything. *Don't be a fool.* Milton sighed. He heard shuffling feet and strained to see Josh burst into the living room, munching on something. He had donned a brown jacket. He paused when he saw Milton reclining on the sofa.

"You're not going?" Josh said, a frown on his face. For someone who had been in a coma, he looked too good. That bothered Milton.

"Of course. I'll go with you." He said as he shot upwards to make his point.

"I hope you're not wearing that to the service." Josh said, pointing at Milton's rumpled trousers. He glanced at his trousers noting for the first time the smudges on it. He hadn't washed in weeks. Lucky for him, he had plenty of pants to choose from. He glanced at the wall clock and gaped in puzzlement.

"Why didn't you wake me up?"

"I thought you needed the sleep. Seems I was right. You were snoring like–. You don't want to know?"

"Let me get a quick shower and we will be on our way. Hey, you didn't finish the rest of the food in the kitchen, did you?" Milton paused at the doorway, waiting for a response from Josh. Josh looked up guiltily at Milton.

"Some things never change." Milton said as he closed the door before Josh could form a witty response.

THE SKIES WERE CLOUDY as Josh and Milton made their way into the church. It was threatening to rain when they found a seat in the pews and waited for the church to fill up. Josh had gone off to a group of his friends. He was a local celebrity now, with everyone fussing over him. Milton glanced at his watch and saw it was a quarter past eight. The church was slowly filling up. The organist was playing the hymn "To God be the Glory." Father Grant was seated in front of the altar, hands clasped in lap as he surveyed the people entering the church. He nodded at Milton when he saw him. A few of the people who had visited Josh at the hospital waved at him.

He began to tap his foot to the rhythm of the hymn being played. Alnight services were not something he really enjoyed. Josh and Milton knew they were both indebted to the church for their support. For that he was willing to sit through the service. He gazed at the statue of Jesus hanging above the altar and felt a twinge of guilt. *I need to confess what I have done.*

"Confess what?" A feminine voice said beside him, causing him to take a sharp breath. *Had he said that out loud?* Trying to hide the embarrassment in his face, he smiled sheepishly at Carol. She raised her brow at him. A part of him twitched at seeing her in that flowery blouse with a black skirt.

"Hey" Milton said, shifting to make way for Carol on the bench.

"It's something, isn't it?" Carol said as she nodded towards where Josh was huddled in between his friends.

"Yeah, it is." Milton replied tonelessly. Carol frowned at him.

"Are you okay?" she asked, with a frown.

"Why do you ask?" Milton tried to give her a reassuring smile.

"You look so—"

Carol's next words were cut off as the priest took the podium and the congregation stood. Carol's stare told him they would have the conversation later. *Did he give anything away?*

"We began this service in the name of the Father..."

Milton went through the motions of the service. His mind was elsewhere. When the praises began, Carol jabbed him in the ribs to dance. He smiled at her and appeased her by moving side to side. She only shook her head at him. When the youth president took center stage, the atmosphere changed. It was a time for a prayer. While Catholics were not known for their charismatic dispositions, a paradigm shift in the church's management had allowed deliverance services to be held. The prayer service started with a string of worship songs Milton was familiar with. Milton did his best to play along, but after some time got bored. Carol had moved out of the pew and was actively praying, moving back and forth. Every single person he looked upon was praying. *Why couldn't he pray?* The priest was seated head bowed. All around him, people were crying out to God, yet he couldn't.

Milton, your soul is mine.

A voice whispered close to him. Dread filled his heart when he heard that voice. Milton turned and stared into the face of a young girl standing beside him. Her face contorted into something akin only in horror movies. He bit back a scream. His heart was walloping against chest, mouth dry. He closed his eyes and opened them again. The young girl stared at Milton in confusion. He must look terrified. He smiled back, trying to calm down his beating heart.

Your soul is mine, boy.

Milton gasped, drawing stares from those around him. He swiveled his head and found everyone still praying. Outside, the rain began in earnest. He vaguely heard the youth leader ask everyone to pray against demonic forces. His panicked gaze travelled round, halting at the statue of Jesus. Cold dread crept up his spine as the bronze figure stared at him. If he was scared, now he felt his legs shaking.

Traitor!

Did he hear that wrong or was he imagining it. He began to hyperventilate. This is not real. Then he heard the voices. He listened closely and felt goose pimples all him.

TRAITOR! DEMON BARGAINER! BLASPHEMER!

Milton backtracked, screaming from terror. The church had gone deadly silent. Josh was staring at him in confusion. Every head was looking at him. His eyes locked gazes with the priest. He saw the understanding in them. He knew. Oh God!

"Milton–"

"I'm sorry." Milton said as he turned and rushed out of the church to obvious murmuring from everyone. He heard the priest calling out his name but was too far gone to turn back. He flung the gates open and stepped into the deluge, nearly blinded from the lightning streaking across the skies. He descended the stairs and in his haste to leave collided into an old woman with a shawl over her head. They both tumbled into the wet sludge. He paused and offered her a helping hand. The wind blew her shawl from her head. Milton gazed into black eyes.

"You're mine, bitch!"

An ancient voice emanated out of the old woman. Milton gasped and fell back from her.

"Your soul is mine, boy." He ran, never glancing back to see that spectacle again. His beating heart was pounding in his ears. He reached the road and flagged down a taxi. He was drenched and heaving his chest out.

"Where to boss?" The driver asked, his face hidden in the shadows.

"Bad day to be out in the rain, boy." A steel voice said, causing Milton's gut to churn in fear.

"What did you say?" Milton said, clearly spooked by the voice. The cab driver didn't answer.

"I said what did you–"

The cab driver hit the brakes suddenly causing Milton to lurch forward and hit his head on the seat. Pain blossomed across his temple. Through the front screen, lightning arced across the sky bathing the night sky in a white light. The driver turned in his seat to face him.

"Did you really think you could escape from me, boy?" Drool dripped from the driver's mouth. Milton's breath hitched as he gazed at the driver's black eyes. He scrambled back, fumbling with the car door. He unlocked it and jumped out, in the car, a deranged laughter was coming from the throat of the driver. Milton stood up, and slipped into a puddle of water. He backed away from the car whose occupant stared at him in confusion.

He run all way to his house and entered. He locked the door behind him. Chest heaving, he slipped to the floor and tried to get his breath. Outside, the downpour still continued, disrupted by the occasional booms of thunder. He slowly lifted himself, and sauntered towards the bedroom. Teeth chattering, he entered and sat on his bed. Arms around himself as his body shook from the cold. He saw the rosary by his bedside and clutched it. Milton breathed slowly to calm his beating heart. He had to end this once and for all. But first he needed to change.

AFTER HE WAS DONE CHANGING, he groped under the bed and his hand latched onto the red book. He pulled it out and gazed upon the cursed thing. He fumbled with his rosary and prayed a silent prayer. He took a lighter from the kitchen and went into the garage. Milton silently prayed for strength for what he was about to do. He picked an old can filled with petrol and poured it on the red book. He heard a howling sound outside. A door banged, momentarily causing him to panic. He fished the lighter out of his pocket and stared at the engraving on it. TRUTH AND PESERVERANCE was scrawled on it. It had been a gift from his father on his fifteen birthday. He ignited it on the book and watched as a blue flame engulfed it. Milton grinned, finally relieving himself of the damned thing. He hoped whatever demon he had unleashed was gone for good. His joy was short lived.

Milton gazed intently at the book as he realized it was intact despite the blue flame sizzling around it.

"No! No!" He felt his heart skyrocketing. His breath came in short pants. He took the can of petrol, and doused the book with more fuel. Maybe the book was made with fire resistant fibers. The flames roiled upwards causing him to stumble backwards and slip to the floor. Milton felt a malevolent presence in the room. Every atom of his body screamed for him to flee yet his body stood rooted to the spot. He gazed in horror at the image in the fire.

"Holy Mother of God. What have I done?" He cried out, a deep unsettling fear overcame him. He felt himself moving towards the fire. Something was pulling him.

YOUR SOUL IS MINE BOY!

Milton knew he was doomed. His mind screamed to God, begging for forgiveness. He felt the searing heat on his face. The malignant face in the fire opened its mouth. He dimly heard the honking of a horn, but took no notice. *Had God abandoned him*? He was going to be damned for wanting his brother to live. A maniacal laughter filled the garage. The face in the fire roiled ready to devour him in a flurry of flames when a hand pushed him away.

"BEGONE DEMON!" The baritone voice of the priest bellowed at the apparition in the flames. It howled in fury.

"I command you, infernal demon to the depths of the abyss where you belong." The white cassock of the priest came into Milton's line of sight. Milton heard a whooshing sound and knew the malignant presence had left. He breathed a sigh of relief. The last thing he saw was Father Grant's wet face as he bent over him and said. "You're safe now, son." Then everything went dark.

NINETEEN

The wind ruffled his black coat as he stood by the graves of his parents. Milton stared at the statue of the Holy Mother erected over the graves. His gaze swept across the cemetery. The plaque on his parents' tomb read: HERE LIES BELOVED HUSBAND AND WIFE. MAY THEIR SOULS REST IN PEACE.

He heard the crunch of boots on leaves as Father Grant came to join him. The priest had done away with his cassock in favour of a black jacket. They both stood silently, basking in the somber solitude the cemetery offered. Each lost in his own thoughts.

"Demons are real." Milton said.

The priest gazed forlornly into the distance, and replied. "We all have our inner demons, Milton." The priest turned his gaze to Milton. "You've a lot in common with your dad. When he was your age, he meddled in things he shouldn't have."

Milton tried to ping in but bit back his tongue.

"I knew about the book. It has been in your family for generations."

"I don't understand."

"You did not read the warnings in the letter."

"No." Milton replied, clearly baffled to the turn of the conversation. The weeks following the incident had been a blur in his mind. He had confessed everything to the priest. He had been shocked when the priest told him that he was aware of the existence of the book and that they were many of such books in existence. This priest indeed had many layers to him.

"There are many mysteries in this world. Maybe one day we will share a drink and I would tell you some of my– interesting tales." The priest said as he patted him on the shoulder and walked away. Milton stood there listening to the receding footsteps of the priest. He glanced to his left and saw Carol and Josh together beckoning him to come over. His parents might be dead, but he still had Josh and Carol. He slowly made his way towards them. He reached them and instinct made him glance towards the graves again. For a moment he thought he saw something, but he dispelled it as his imagination getting the best of him.

"Hey bro, everything alright?" Josh asked.

"Just thinking what a great day it is."

"Yeah, one to go dancing right?" Josh said, glancing mischievously between his brother and Carol who was blushing. Milton shook his head as they both burst out laughing. They would be alright. At least his soul would be safe now.

"Come on. Let's get out of here." The three walked out of the cemetery, leaving the Holy Mother in her hunch like pose guarding the tombs of their parents.

THE END

Don't miss out!

Visit the website below and you can sign up to receive emails whenever N.K. Aning publishes a new book. There's no charge and no obligation.

https://books2read.com/r/B-A-WWEE-LREP

BOOKS 2 READ

Connecting independent readers to independent writers.

Did you love *The Conjuring*? Then you should read *Damned* by N.K. Aning!

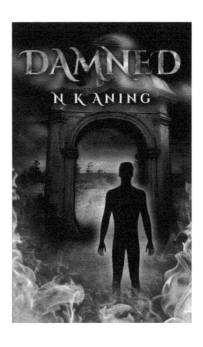

Edward had been a man of faith, always believing in the unfailing love of his creator. But when he ends up at the gate of hell, he begins to wonder if the God he had been taught to believe in was ever real..

Michaella was not a believer in God. But when fate pulls them together into the dark recesses of hell, they discover an explosive truth which would change their lives forever.

For even in hell, there is redemption for those who search for it.

Read more at https://web.facebook.com/ N-K-Aning-879564645456623/?view_public_for=879564645456623.

Also by N.K. Aning

The Bronze Man's Secret
Damned
Prophecy
The Conjuring
In Her Eyes
The Addiction
The God Dilemma
Jack and God
Jason And The Great Dragon
A Song for Eyram
The Infernal Jury
Pierce and the City of Imaginaterium

Watch for more at https://web.facebook.com/
N-K-Aning-879564645456623/?view_public_for=879564645456623.

CPSIA information can be obtained
at www.ICGtesting.com
Printed in the USA
BVHW060007111121
621201BV00008B/525

9 781393 252702